ROLLING OUT A MYSTERY

CHRISTIAN COZY MYSTERY

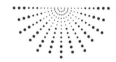

DONNA DOYLE

© 2018 PUREREAD LTD

CONTENTS

INTRODUCTION

A PERSONAL WORD FROM PUREREAD

 Dear reader,

Do you love a good mystery? So do we! Nothing is more pleasing than a page turner that keeps you guessing until the very last page.

In our Christian cozy mysteries you can be certain that there won't be any gruesome or gory scenes, swearing or anything else upsetting, just good clean fun as you unravel the mystery together with our marvelous characters.

Thank you for choosing PureRead!

A Warm Welcome From Donna Doyle

To find out more about PureRead mysteries and receive new release information and other goodies from Donna Doyle go to our website
PureRead.com/donnadoyle

Enjoy The Story!

GATHER YOUR INGREDIENTS

Sammy Baker expertly assembled a large box with a clear window on the top, filled it with twelve cinnamon rolls from her latest batch, and brought it out to the front of the café. Now that it was October and the weather was turning cooler, the customers at Just Like Grandma's were flooding in the doors for Helen's homemade soups and Sammy's freshly baked goods. She had taken her friend's advice and started selling them by the box instead of just individually, and there were plenty of customers who came in simply to buy a box to take to the office.

"That'll be \$8.95," Helen said from behind the cash register as she handed a box over the counter to the patron she was ringing up. "Oh, Sammy! Please tell me you've got more cinnamon rolls out there!"

"I do. I was just going to put them on the table with the... others?" The back corner of the dining area had been repurposed into a makeshift bakery display with a small table for the boxes of goods, but it was currently empty. "Where did everything go?"

"Where do you think?" Helen asked with a laugh as she handed over the customer's change. "We can't keep them in stock for anything. I've sold every box, and I've had at least five other people asking if there are more. You have more in the back?"

Sammy shrugged helplessly. "This batch should make up another couple of boxes, but that's it. I'll have to get more going, and it will take some time since they have to rise. But I'm behind on washing dishes, and I've hardly been out on the floor to help with serving." She surveyed the packed tables and sighed, wishing she could clone herself.

"Well, if it's the tips you're worried about, I think you're making plenty off of your baked goods. And if it's me you're worried about?" Helen raised an eyebrow but let out a cackling laugh as she swung her long, gray braid over her shoulder. "I can handle these folks. They don't scare me. Isn't that right, Blake?"

The young man who had just paid for his meal wore a dark blue jumpsuit with the logo for A-1 Auto emblazoned on the back. He smiled sweetly at Helen. "That's right, ma'am. Anything you say."

"I've got you trained well, young man! Now get yourself on to work before your boss yells at you. Go on!" She immediately turned to the next customer lined up at the counter.

Biting her lower lip, Sammy dashed to the back to start the next batch of rolls. Once she had them formed and rising, she came back out to the front to help Helen with the customers. As she worked, she realized just how happy she was. Moving back to Sunny Cove hadn't been part of her original plan, but neither had getting divorced from a cheating husband. When she found herself leaving New York and coming home, she felt like such an outsider after all the years she had been gone. But it was starting to feel like home again as she got to know the people in this small town once again, and now she knew how they liked their coffee and their eggs.

The only thing that she felt was missing a little in her life was going to church on Sunday mornings. She had considered it several times since she had arrived, and once she had even gotten dressed and ready to go. Church had been such a big part of her life when she was younger, and she didn't know if she could quite step back into it. She had set aside those beliefs when her father had been falsely accused of fraud and money laundering, and Sammy was discovering that it was far easier to stop going than to start going back.

A familiar face stepped through the door. His dark curls had been blown around by the October breeze, and his green eyes were wild with excitement. In khaki pants and a strange looking top that looked like it had been part of some sort of costume, there was no mistaking the distinct fashion sense of Austin Absher. "Sammy!" he exclaimed as he came in the door, spreading his arms wide and making the entire restaurant turn to look at him.

"Hi, Austin. Why don't you come have a seat at the counter?" Sammy gestured toward an open stool, knowing that if she didn't direct the man he was likely to make trouble for himself. Austin was a grown man, but his mental disability often kept him from behaving himself.

"I'm hungry," he replied as he sat. "The first peanut butter machine was invented in 1904."

"That's very interesting. I had no idea. Is that what you'd like? A peanut butter and jelly sandwich?"

Austin bobbed his head eagerly. "And milk!"

"Coming right up!"

Helen gave her a look as she came around the counter and headed to the kitchen.

"Don't worry. It's coming out of my pay," Sammy promised her boss. "The least I can do is buy the poor boy a sandwich every now and then."

"I know, and I understand. But people are like stray cats. You give them something for free, and they start expecting it all the time. I just don't want to see you getting taken advantage of." The older woman grabbed a rag to mop up a sticky spot on a nearby table. "You know I've done what I could to help Austin in the past, but I just don't think there's much hope for him."

"He hasn't stolen anything in at least two weeks," Sammy pointed out, but the point she had hoped to make fell flat even to her ears once she heard it come out. "Look, you have to admit that he's done well. He used to constantly be in trouble with the law and chase your customers away. But I made him promise to behave himself, and he's done well." Her heart had gone out to him since the first time she had met him, when he had run away from Sheriff Jones and straight into the kitchen at Just Like Grandma's.

"He's got an affinity for you, that's for sure. Maybe baking isn't your only talent." Helen poured a mug of coffee and slid it down the counter toward a man in a flannel shirt.

"I think he just needs something to look forward to. He comes in here every day, gets a little bit of food, and he gets to talk to you or me for a few minutes. It doesn't sound as though he has a very good home life, and I think he likes to get out and socialize. Hey, maybe if he had a job!" Sammy snapped her fingers as the thought came to her, wondering why she hadn't come up with the idea before.

"I don't know that there's much he could do."

"Sure there is!" They had a dining room full of customers, but the only one who mattered to Sammy at the moment was Austin. The rest of them could take care of themselves, after all. "What if he washed dishes and swept the floors around here? Or took out the trash? It wouldn't have to be anything difficult, and we wouldn't do anything with food for money."

"Sammy, honey." Helen put her hands on Sammy's upper arms and leveled her dark eyes at her. "Don't get too far ahead of yourself. I tried that once. It's more than the boy can handle, and he needs someone to supervise him constantly. You know I like to help out where I can—and I can tell you right now that the sandwich you're about to make him is certainly not coming out of your pay—but there's a limit to charity when you run your own business."

Sammy felt her shoulders sag a little. "Oh, I didn't realize. That's too bad. I think a job would be so good for him."

Helen patted her on the shoulder. "Don't look so disheartened, child. You're doing what you can, and that's a lot more than most even bother to think about. Now, go make that sandwich and check on those cinnamon rolls. I've seen several customers looking toward the pastry table."

Doing as she was told, Sammy made sure she spent a few moments with Austin where she could between the paying customers. He was a sweet boy who just wanted some friends, and it didn't seem fair to her that he had been excluded because of a disorder. Maybe if he'd been given a few more chances in life, he wouldn't be dressing in mismatched castoffs that the thrift stores wouldn't take and stealing food.

She was just about to finish up her shift when Heather Girtman strutted in. She didn't bother taking a seat, choosing to lounge against the counter instead. "Good morning, sunshine!" she purred.

"You know it's well past noon, right?" Sammy had been

friends with Heather in high school, but they had both changed a lot since then.

Heather flicked her long nails in the air. "It's not like it matters. Now, tell me you don't have anything going on Saturday night. I know you don't, because you never have any plans."

Sammy couldn't help but feel a little insulted at this, even though it was true. "Just unpacking a few more boxes, but that's about it."

"Oh, you're so boring!" Heather rolled her blue eyes. "I'll fix that. There's a big Halloween party at Rob Hewitt's house this weekend. *Everyone* is going to be there, including a ton of people we went to school with."

"I don't know." Sammy hadn't ever been much of a fan of Halloween. "I'm not sure about celebrating ghosts and ghouls."

"You're thinking about it too much," Heather replied. "It's just an excuse for people to get together and have a little fun. And it'll be *extra* fun since it's a costume party and not everyone knows you're back in Sunny Cove. You've got to come!"

Sammy pulled in a breath, preparing to explain that she really couldn't. She had too many other things to do. But the truth was that the only socializing she'd done since she'd returned had been through her work. She talked to her customers, and she and Heather had dinner a couple of times, but that was about it. If she was truly going to be happy here, she was going to need more of a life than that. "Well, I guess I could. I don't have anything to wear, though."

"Just go buy something from the store. It doesn't have to be special. I'm going to be a pirate, so just don't copy me." Heather winked and straightened up. "I'll see you there at eight on Saturday!" She bounced out of the café without giving Sammy the chance to change her mind.

2

PREHEAT OVEN

Sammy looked at herself in the full-length mirror on the back of the bathroom door, wondering if she should have picked out a better costume. But when she had gone to the shop over in Oak Hills, it had been hard enough just finding something that didn't have an incredibly short skirt or a revealing top. Instead, Sammy had settled on a long pink poodle skirt, a black button-up top, and saddle shoes. She had always loved the idea of the fifties, when the times seemed simpler, and the costume was cute and conservative. It would just have to be good enough. She pulled her blonde waves up into a ponytail, tied a little scarf around it, and went downstairs to her car.

It was easy to find the address Heather had given her over the phone a couple days ago when she had called to not only remind Sammy of the party but to make sure she was actually coming. Rob Hewitt lived in his parents' old house, a massive structure on the edge of town, far away from any of the smaller homes where most people lived. Cars were parked up and down both sides of the road, and Sammy had to park almost a block away. She touched the tote bag in the passenger seat next to her, which contained jeans and a t-shirt just in case Heather had been pulling her leg about this being a costume party. But other folks were streaming down the sidewalk in capes, masks, and elaborate dresses.

Sammy flipped down her visor and stared herself down in the mirror. "You can do this," she reminded herself. "Like Heather said, it doesn't matter if it's a Halloween party. It's a chance to get to know people again. And you need that, even if it seems hard." She took a deep breath and got out of the car.

When she made it into the living room, Heather found her right away. "You made it! You know, I really thought you were going to chicken out on me." She was dressed in a pirate costume as she had promised, complete with a short, tight dress in red and black with lace trim.

Sammy doubted that any pirates wore much lace, but she knew that wasn't the point. "I wouldn't miss it," she replied with a forced smile.

Her old friend didn't notice her discomfort. "Look, there's Jamie Stewart over there in the nurse costume. Oh, and Sarah Jacobs is over there talking to Andrea Probst. Do you remember them?" Heather grabbed Sammy by the arm and led her around the room, pointing people out and talking about them, but never bothering to walk up to them and start a conversation.

"Heather Girtman, as I live and breathe!" said a snarky voice behind them.

Sammy and Heather turned as one to find Lindsay Thompson standing there, Allison and Gracie at her sides. It was just like it had been back in school, when the most popular girl spent all her time harassing everyone else with her two best friends at her sides.

"Lindsay," Heather sneered. "How *very nice* to see you."

"Right." Lindsay's eyes scraped over Sammy's costume. "Very original. I've had mine since August, you know."

Sammy's face burned as she realized that her getup was almost identical to Lindsay's. It looked, though, like the other woman had sprung for the deluxe costume, one made of quality fabrics that could have been authentic. But there was no apology she could make for grabbing something off the store shelf like everyone else had, so she simply shrugged.

Lindsay probably wouldn't have noticed even if Sammy'd had a good comeback. "If this was my house, I'd kick you out," she said to Heather. "As it is, I suggest you keep your hands to yourself."

"There has to be something worth laying them on before I can worry about it," Heather retorted, hands on her hips and shoulders back. "Maybe you should grow up a little, Lindsay. Bye." She turned away, bringing Sammy with her.

"What was that all about?" Sammy was aggravated with herself for being so meek around Lindsay. She might have been popular back in school, but they had graduated a long time ago. None of that should matter now.

Heather tossed her raven locks. "Who knows? She's always got something stuck in her craw. We should just have fun. Let's go get a drink!"

"Um, you go ahead. I see someone I'd like to talk to." Sammy moved to the other side of the room, where a tall man in a sheriff's uniform stood near the wall, surveying the crowd. "That's not a very inventive costume," she joked.

Sheriff Jones looked down at her with a smile. "I just got off work, and I didn't see much point in dressing up when I know I'm not going to stay long. I have to go to court first thing in the morning. You look nice, though."

Sammy felt her cheeks heat up. "Thanks. I'm glad I ran into you. There's something I'd like to work on, and I thought you might have some ideas for me."

"Oh?" He raised a thin eyebrow, his dark blue eyes sparkling.

"You see, I really want to do something to help Austin Absher." Sammy hadn't been able to get him off her mind for the last several days. She had never met someone who called to her heart like this, and she knew she had to find some way to help him get a better life. "Are there any places around here who employ people like him? I think it would keep him from stealing, and maybe he could earn some extra money for food."

"Here we go again," the sheriff mumbled. "Look Sammy, this isn't the big city. Programs like what you're talking about take a lot of money and effort. The churches do what they can for local charities, but they can't do much more than provide winter clothes and maybe a few canned goods for the needy."

"But that means that we *need* those kinds of programs," Sammy argued. "I'm sure Austin isn't the only one who's struggling. I asked Helen about having him work at Just Like Grandma's, but she said that's too much for him. You seem to know him well. Have any ideas?"

Jones ran a hand through his close-cropped hair. "I'm afraid I don't. I've done what I can, bringing him to the station for coffee or giving him a ride when he needs it. But Austin has really built a reputation for himself around here, and it isn't a good one. You're going to have a hard time getting anyone else on board."

Sammy felt so disappointed. "Okay, thanks anyway. If you think of anything, you know where to find me." She headed over to the drinks table to see if Heather was still around.

There were no pirates in sight, so Sammy looked through the available drink choices until she found a cold can of Coke.

"Just go easy on the rum tonight. You made enough of a

fool of yourself at the last party, and you're lucky I let you come again."

"Excuse me?" Sammy turned to the man standing next to her.

His pale green eyes widened in surprise when he looked back at her. "Oh, I'm sorry! I thought you were someone else. Samantha Beaumont, right?"

"Well, it's Baker now, but yeah."

"Oh, I didn't realize you were married." Rob Hewitt, the host of the party and the former star of the football team, scooped some ice into a red plastic cup and filled it with Sprite. He was dressed as Robin Hood, but he had thrown the hood back and slung his bow over his shoulder.

Sammy regretted keeping her married name, because it meant she always had something to explain. "I'm divorced now."

"I'm sorry. I didn't realize."

"There's no need to be sorry. I've been out of Sunny Cove for a long time, and I wouldn't expect anyone to keep up with every little thing I've done." Rob swirled the soda in his cup. "I stayed here because my father wanted me to take over his law practice. It's not been a bad thing, but sometimes I wish I could have gotten away and seen the world."

Several more people filed in the front door, but Sammy still couldn't find Heather anywhere. "Have you seen

Heather? I came with her, but she disappeared a few minutes ago."

"Heather's here?" Rob looked startled. "I didn't know. I haven't seen her."

"Okay. I'm going to find her. It was nice to see you again!" Sammy raised her Coke and moved off, hoping she looked more enthusiastic than she felt. Rob had always been a big jock and they had never known each other all that well in school, but he was a nice guy. Still, she didn't feel very comfortable here and was ready to leave. She couldn't very well do that without letting Heather know first.

But her pirate friend had unexpectedly disappeared. She checked the kitchen and the hallway and found plenty of ghosts and witches, but no Heather. Finally, she stopped to ask Lindsay, who rolled her eyes and laughed.

"It's not my job to keep track of her. But yeah, I saw her having yet another fight with Billy York. No idea what happened to her after that." She didn't have her two friends with her for a change. Lindsay held her drink in one hand and fiddled with the material of her skirt with the other.

"Thanks." Sammy wasn't sure what she should do. She didn't want to be rude and leave the party without talking to Heather, since this had all been her idea anyway, but she was ready to go home and relax for a while. She was just turning toward the front door when a scream pierced the din of the crowd.

Everyone looked to the stairs, and a woman with curly brown hair came rushing down. Sammy recognized her as Jamie Stewart. She had been the lead role in every play that Sunny Cove High School had put on. "There's blood all over the upstairs bathroom!" she hollered out to the crowd. "It's disgusting!"

Sheriff Jones was now moving through the crowd toward her. "Is anyone hurt?"

"I don't know! You go look!" She ran down to the landing and pointed up the stairs as though a monster was after her.

Jones trotted up the stairs. The crowd waited anxiously, and someone had turned off the music. He returned a few minutes later, muttering into his radio. "All right, folks. It looks like we might have a situation on our hands, so I need everyone to remain calm. Does anybody recognize this?" He held up a red and black scrap of fabric that he had picked up with a tissue.

A wave of horror crept over Sammy's skin. "That looks like part of Heather's costume."

He nodded, his mouth a firm line. "Folks, I've got some other officers on the way. I'm going to clear out this house, but first I need the names and phone numbers of everyone here. If you could form a nice neat line near the front door, it would be helpful."

The attendees obeyed orders, but they didn't do it quietly. Sammy stood in line, biting her lip and shifting her weight from foot to foot. She was relieved when she finally made her way to the sheriff. "Is there anything I can do to help?"

Sheriff Jones had proven to be friendly when he wanted to be, but right now he was in the middle of an investigation. "Absolutely not. I just need your phone number so I can contact you if I need a statement, but I don't want anyone to get involved in this."

She nodded, but she wasn't happy about it. "Will you let me know if you find out anything? I'm worried about her."

His sapphire eyes softened slightly. "I'll see what I can do."

3

MELT A STICK OF BUTTER

I t was difficult to return to work the next day, not knowing what had happened to Heather. But Sammy knew that it wasn't going to do anyone any good if she just sat around in her apartment and pretended to be sick all day, and she knew Helen was counting on her. She showered and dragged herself down the stairs to work, throwing herself into her baking to keep her mind distracted. She churned out several more batches of cinnamon rolls, since they just couldn't seem to keep them in stock, and then she concentrated on several loaves of bread. One or two would get sliced up and served with Helen's soups, and the remainder would be wrapped and set out on the pastry table. Sammy had a feeling they would be gone before noon.

She had just placed her last two loaves in the oven when Helen poked her head in the kitchen. "Sammy, there's someone at the counter who would like to see you."

Her heart thundered nervously as she dusted flour off her

hands and pushed through the swinging door, imagining that Sheriff Jones had come to give her an update. But the woman at the counter who looked so hopefully at her was definitely not Sheriff Jones.

"Hi, Sammy. I don't know if you remember me. I'm Valerie Girtman, Heather's mom." She was a plump woman of middle age, but she was only an older version of Heather. Her dark hair was starting to go gray, and her eyes were a lighter shade of blue than her daughter's.

Sammy hadn't spent a lot of time at Heather's house, but there was no mistaking the resemblance. "Of course, I remember you. What can I do for you?" Again, she held out hope that there was good news coming her way. Maybe Jones had talked to Valerie and asked her to pass along a message.

Heather's mother leaned her elbows on the counter and wrung her hands together. "I was just hoping you might have heard something from Heather. She had told me the two of you were going to that party together. I don't like that she goes out so much, but I thought it would be all right since you were going to be there. But she never came home last night, and Sheriff Jones came by the house to tell me part of her costume had been found. I'm so worried about her, Sammy. I don't know what to do." Tears swelled in her eyes.

Sammy came around the counter to put her arm around the older woman. "I'm so sorry. I don't know anything, either. I've been thinking about her all day, though. I'm sure we're all just overthinking it. That's what Heather is always telling me, anyway."

Valerie nodded and sniffled. "I hope you're right. Things haven't been very easy on Heather, you know. She just always seems to be making the wrong decisions. She was like that even when she was a kid. I had hoped she would grow out of it, but now I'm not so sure she ever will. She had even moved back in with me because she couldn't afford to pay her own rent anymore. I told her she could as long as she kept herself on the straight and narrow, but now all I do is sit at home and worry about her because I don't know where she is or what she's doing." She paused, looking uncertain. "I'm worried that something might have happened to her, but I also have to admit that this isn't the first time something like this has happened. She goes out on the weekend, and then she just decides to stay somewhere without telling me about it. I just want her to have a good life, you know?"

Reaching behind the counter to grab a tissue, Sammy replied, "I know. I'm really sorry I don't know anything more."

"That's all right, sweetheart." Valerie patted her hand. "I have to tell you I was so relieved when Heather told me you were back in town. You were always such a good influence on Heather, and I hope that it will continue. Maybe you can get through to Heather in ways that I can't."

Sammy appreciated the compliment, but she also felt as though Heather's wellbeing was entirely her responsibility now. But nobody could expect her to make Heather do a full about-face in an instant. "The two of us aren't as close as we used to be," she admitted, "but it's been nice to get to know her again."

"You'll have to come to the house for dinner some night. Well, I'd better get going. I have a few more people on my list to talk to today." She slid off the stool gracelessly.

"The sheriff is letting you help?" Sammy asked, realizing as she said it what a silly question it was. "Sorry, it's just that he told me I wasn't to get involved when I asked if there was anything I could do."

Valerie gave her a watery smile and patted her arm. "Oh, honey. Sheriff Jones can say whatever he wants, but I'm her mother. I'm going to do anything and everything I can until my little girl comes back home."

"Good luck. I'll be sure to call you if I hear anything."

"Thank you, dear."

Sammy watched her go, suddenly feeling much more connected to her little community than she had in a long time. Even if she didn't think she belonged, it was clear that there were others who needed her. Austin was one of them, and now so was Heather.

4

MIX IN THE SUGAR

Sammy didn't sleep well that night. She had a very comfortable mattress, and the apartment above Just Like Grandma's was a clean and cozy one. But every time she closed her eyes, her mind started working on the problems of Heather and Austin. They were completely separate issues, but they equally demanded her attention. She constantly saw images of Heather in that pirate costume, and the scrap of cheap cloth that had been torn from it and covered in blood. She would wake and roll over, reminding herself that she couldn't do anything about it until morning, but then she would dream of Austin, wondering what would become of him if she didn't take steps to help.

She was relieved when her alarm went off in the morning. She hadn't gotten nearly enough sleep, and that was going to make for a long day, but it was too much of a frustrating effort to do anything but get up and hop in the shower. She made a cup of strong coffee and vowed to make the most of her day.

Firing up the oven first thing, Sammy started with her pastries. The cinnamon rolls had once again been depleted, and so she started a batch of those before moving on to biscuits and rolls. She hadn't even taken the cinnamon rolls out of the oven before Helen stepped into the kitchen to see if she had any available, and the first dozen were sold individually to customers who were dining in.

The breakfast rush was just beginning to slow down when Austin came in, looking hopeful. He sat at the counter without being prompted and stared at Sammy until she had time to come around to him.

"How are you today, Austin?"

"Not very good," he admitted quietly.

This gave her pause. It was rare that he answered any question with something other than enthusiasm or a random fact. "Why's that?"

"I'm very hungry," he admitted.

"You know I'll get something for you. Don't you have any food at home?" She had avoided asking about his home life too much, because it seemed to be such a touchy subject with everyone else in Sunny Cove. But maybe she wasn't giving him enough credit.

"The fridge has three packets of ketchup, half a bottle of

mustard, a jar of pickles and a plastic container with mold in it. Penicillin was discovered in 1928." His eyes lit up a little at finding another historical fact to tell her.

"I'll try to remember that. You know, Austin, I've been thinking about you a lot. I think what you need is a job." She watched him carefully, unsure of how he would react. He had been known to be volatile sometimes, and Sammy didn't know him as well as Helen or Sheriff Jones did.

"A job?" he echoed. "Here?"

"No, not here. I think we need to find something that suits you better."

"Like what?"

Sammy lifted one shoulder and let it fall. "I'm not sure. That's why I need your help. Tell me what you like to do, and maybe I can help you find a job that's right for you." She didn't say that she would also have to find a place that was willing to hire him, since he wasn't someone that everyone in Sunny Cove was willing to deal with. She would figure that part out for herself.

"What I like to do? Nobody's ever asked me that." He looked off into the distance as though he would find the answer there.

"That's okay. You think about it for a minute, and I'll get you something to eat." She trotted back to the kitchen, fixing up a couple of plates that other customers had ordered and delivering them before getting Austin the last cinnamon roll and a cup of coffee.

"I like to watch TV," he finally said when she came back.

There were no jobs that would let him just sit around and watch TV all day, but it was a start. "What kind of shows do you like to watch?"

"Documentaries," he answered instantly.

Sammy nodded. It made perfect sense, considering he was always spouting off random information. "I should have guessed that. Is there anything else you like to do? Or that you're good at? Do you know how to clean?"

Austin scrunched up his face. "Uncle Mitch doesn't clean much. There are seven cobwebs in the bathroom."

"I see. Hmmm." This wasn't going very well. She tapped her fingers against her cheek as she turned to look out the window, trying to think. The autumn breeze was in full swing for the day, sending a balled-up newspaper rolling down the sidewalk. Maybe she didn't need to rely on Austin being capable of any sort of skilled labor. "Do you think you could pick up trash on the side of the road?"

"People throw away seven pounds of trash every day," Austin recited.

"That's terrible, and I know that it doesn't all make it into the trash can. How would you feel if someone paid you to pick up trash?"

His eyes lit up in a way Sammy hadn't seen before. "I'd love it!"

"Great! You give me some time, and I'll find you a job doing just that, okay?"

"Okay!" Austin realized the food was in front of him, and he dug into the cinnamon roll. "This is good, Sammy."

"Thank you." She was feeling excited about the prospect of finding Austin a job. There might not be many people who would be willing to let him into their business, but surely they would let him work outside. Maybe he could also rake leaves or pick up fallen branches, but she would have to start with one thing at a time. And Austin's most immediate concern needed to be his empty stomach. "Do you know when your Uncle Mitch is going to go shopping? To get you some food?"

"Every time he flips the calendar," he replied eagerly, bobbing his head and glad that he knew the answer to something.

But that meant there was still a week until the first of November, and Austin wouldn't have any food in his house. "I tell you what. There are some leftovers in the back. I'll package them up for you and you can take them home. You can share with Uncle Mitch, too." She hurried into the kitchen before she started to cry at the thought of anybody going without food.

Austin's eyes lit up when she presented him with a bag of containers. "You get on home and make sure your uncle gets some food. And make sure he knows that you didn't steal it. I gave it to you because I want you to have it, okay?"

He nodded. "When do I get to pick up trash?"

Her heart went out to him. She wanted so badly to change his situation, but she had to remember that she was only one person. "As soon as I find someone who can pay you. I'll let you know as soon as I do. Can you write down your phone number for me?"

He had a memory like nobody she had ever met before, and so of course it was no problem for Austin to remember his own phone number. He scribbled it out in childlike handwriting on a piece of paper and trotted out the door, his bag of food in hand.

That evening, just as Sammy sat down with a notebook and a pen, a knock came at her door. It was Helen with a vase of flowers. "I happened to be walking past the florist's this evening, and I saw this in the window. I thought the pale blue of the vase would go wonderfully with your apartment."

"Oh, thank you so much!" Sammy was flabbergasted that her boss would do something like this for her. "You've already done so much for me, including giving me a job and an apartment to rent."

"And you've done quite a lot for me, too," Helen said with a smile. "I like knowing that I have a good person up here instead of just some random transient who will trash the place and then move on. And you have no idea what an addition you've been to the restaurant! I don't think I've ever seen the place so busy, and I'm sure it's because of all the delicious things you make."

"I can't be making that much of a difference," Sammy demurred as she cleared a spot on the coffee table for the vase.

"Yes, you are!" Helen insisted. "No reason to be shy about it! I'm thrilled, that's for sure."

"Well, I wish I could figure out how to make a difference in other ways." Sammy sat down in front of her notebook once again. While she had been at work, she had been excited to come up with ideas for helping Austin, but now the task seemed daunting.

"You're still thinking about that boy, aren't you?" Helen shook her head and clucked her tongue as she took the chair next to Sammy. "You're a sweet girl, and I admire you for being so charitable. But you already work a lot of long hours. How are you going to have time to do this?"

"Well, here's my idea. If I can get a few people to hire Austin on the weekends or evenings to pick up trash or maybe rake some leaves, then he'll have some money in his pocket. Helen, he told me this morning that they didn't have any food in the house and that his uncle wasn't getting paid until the first of the month. I know a lot of people try to make themselves sound worse off than they are to get a handout, but I don't think Austin is capable of that. The poor guy was genuinely hungry, and I imagine his uncle is, too."

"I see." Helen's lips worked together as she thought, her eyes studying the wood grain of the table. "And if he had a job, then he'd have money in his pocket to buy food, and food is what he's always been caught stealing."

"You've got it," Sammy answered. "He's really excited about it, too. I just have to come up with ways to *find* him those jobs, since nobody wants to hire him as an official employee."

"You know, back before I ran this place, I used to do a lot of telemarketing jobs. I found that it really paid off to be prepared before you called someone, that way you could answer any questions that they might have without hesitation. You need to know when Austin is available, how much he's going to charge, and what he's capable of doing. You also need to know if he'll charge different rates for businesses and homes, because there might be a few citizens who would be willing to let him do a little work." She stood up and went to the bookshelf to retrieve a phone book. "I know people don't use these for anything but propping up a table leg these days, but I promise they're still useful."

"This is great!" Sammy squealed, thrilled that Helen was on board. "Maybe I could make up some flyers."

"Don't get too far ahead of yourself," Helen warned. "Flyers cost a lot of money if you're going to print enough of them to really reach people. What about printing out some business cards for him? It doesn't have to be anything special."

The two women went to work, discussing plans and making notes. Sammy felt a little guilty that Austin wasn't in on this part of the planning, but he would still be reaping the rewards later. They wouldn't need to have very many people willing to hire him in order to keep him out of trouble and happy. Sammy grabbed her laptop, found a business card template on her word processor, and had some cards printing out in just a few minutes. Ideas were hitting her left and right, and she had to set down the cards to write them all down before she forgot them. "You know, he could shovel snow during the winter. By then, he would probably have enough money saved up to buy a shovel. Or maybe the Tool Shed would be willing to sponsor him and give him one!"

"That's the spirit!" Helen flipped a page in the phone book and jotted down another business name. "I'm glad to see you happy again. It's a welcome change from the way you looked when you first walked into work. I guess they haven't found anything out about Heather yet?"

"You heard about that?" Sammy had gotten so involved in their plans for Austin that she had actually managed to forget about Heather for a moment. She felt bad about it, but worrying wouldn't help the situation, either.

"Everyone in Sunny Cove has heard about it," Helen assured her. "You should know that."

"You're right. There were a ton of people at that party, and people like to run their mouths around here anyway. I'm sure I'm going to regret asking you this, but are you doing anything to assist in the investigation this time?"

Sammy shook her head. "I asked Sheriff Jones if I could

help. It sounds like I'm the only real friend Heather has anymore, according to her mom. But he said he doesn't want anyone to get mixed up in it. My hands are tied."

"I suppose that's true," Helen mused, a sparkle in her dark eyes.

"And really, we don't even know if Heather is actually missing. Her mom said she goes out and stays gone all the time, so there's always a chance she doesn't want to be found. It's kind of rude of her, since everyone is so concerned, but I feel like I'm stepping in where I don't belong." It was just another aspect of the whole incident that she was constantly wrestling with, and she didn't know how to handle it.

"And you wouldn't want to interfere." Helen echoed her thoughts.

"No. And I have enough going on with Austin. I'm sure I'll need to talk to a lot of people before I find someone who's willing to hire him."

"You'll need a whole list," Helen agreed.

"Wait a minute." Sammy slapped her palm on the table. "I don't want to just go around the neighborhood, surveying every house to see if anyone has seen Heather. But I *have* to go around and talk to people about Austin. Maybe I can get both done at the same time! I'll see if they need any yard work, and then I can casually ask them if they know anything about Heather! It even gives me a list of people to start with, since I can just go talk to the people who were at the party!"

Helen handed over the pen and paper. "Start writing! It's a shame you can't get the information on everyone who attended the party from Sheriff Jones. I don't imagine he would just hand that over to you, not unless there was some sort of connection between the two of you?"

Sammy had started with the list of names, but she paused to look up at her boss. "What's that supposed to mean?"

"Oh, you know," Helen said with a grin. "I see the way the two of you look at each other. Alfie is a good man. You could do much worse than to spend a little time with him."

The skin on Sammy's cheeks burned, and she looked down at her paper again so she wouldn't have to see the way Helen was watching her. "He seems very nice, but I don't think I'm interested in anything like that. I've only been divorced for a couple of months, and I'm not ready to start dating again."

"Right. You need time to find yourself and remember who you are and all that business."

"Yes. Exactly." It was what all the books and online articles recommended, and it all made perfect sense. But now that she had said it out loud, she had to wonder just how accurate that advice was. Maybe it wouldn't hurt to see how things went with a man like Sheriff Jones. But no, it was far too soon.

"I'm sure that's the smart way to do things, and it's certainly the modern one." Helen leaned back in her chair and looked up at the ceiling. "But sometimes it's not so bad to just dive in with both feet and see what happens. I've known far too many women who said they would take a break from men after they got their hearts stomped on, and before they knew it a break turned into a permanent vacation."

Sammy wondered if Helen was talking about herself, but she didn't want to pry. "I'll certainly keep it in mind, but I don't think I'm ready yet. I haven't even been able to get myself to church, and it's something I've really been thinking about a lot lately."

Helen reached across the table and patted her hand. "That's probably the best step to take, dear. If you want someone to go with you, then you know where to find me. For now, I'd better be getting to bed. I'm sure we'll have another busy day tomorrow!" She stood up and headed for the door.

"I really appreciate your help with all of this, Helen," Sammy said sincerely as she showed her out. "I think Austin needs our help more than anyone in this town realizes, and he's so excited. I don't want to let him down."

Helen winked. "You won't, dear. Good night."

5

ADD A PINCH OF SALT

Sammy's stomach churned as she drove across town. She had gotten up and gotten ready for work early so that she would have a little bit of time to start talking to people about Austin and the services he could offer.

Her list was a thorough one. Long after Helen had left, Sammy had sat at the table and written down every single person she could think of who had been at the party. Every time she thought she was done and was just about to set down her pen, she thought of someone else. Many of the partygoers had been people she'd gone to high school with, so even if she hadn't talked to them in a long time, she still knew their names. It wasn't exactly the method Sammy would have preferred for reintroducing herself to her fellow graduates, but it would just have to do.

Lindsay Thompson lived in a big house on the edge of town, not too far from Rob Hewitt's place. Sammy shuddered as she rolled slowly past the place where she had last seen Heather, wondering if the sheriff was making any progress. When she lived in New York, the police departments had a lot more crime to keep up with, but they also had a lot more funding and resources. Was Sheriff Jones up to the task of a missing person? Had he called in any other law enforcement agencies, like maybe the state troopers, to help? Shouldn't someone have organized a search party?

But she drove on past until she found the address that had been listed for Lindsay, parking on the street. Grabbing one of the business cards she had made for Austin, she walked up toward the front door.

It opened before she even stepped up onto the porch. Lindsay's face showed surprise and then disgust before she turned around to lock the door behind her. In her hounds-tooth skirt suit and heels, she was obviously going to work. "What are you doing here?"

Sammy had expected a negative reaction, and she wasn't going to let that get to her or affect her presentation. "Hey, Lindsay. I know we just saw each other a couple days ago, but I didn't actually get a chance to introduce myself. I mean, we went to school together, but it's been a long time." All the words she had carefully rehearsed were getting jumbled on her tongue, and Sammy was concerned that she sounded like a fool.

"I know who you are, Sammy." Lindsay adjusted her bag on her shoulder and curled her upper lip slightly. "What do you want?"

"There's a person in town who really needs some help. You probably know him. His name is Austin Absher, and I'm trying to help him get a few odd jobs so he can earn a little money." Sammy knew that Lindsay's yard was already immaculate. It was hard to imagine she did any of the work herself, which meant she had already hired a landscaping company to keep the grass trimmed.

"Ha!" Lindsay flashed a smile, but it wasn't a friendly one. "Of course I know Austin Absher. Everyone in town knows him, and it's not a good thing. He's got quite the reputation, and it's pretty audacious of him to even think about asking anyone for help after everything he's done."

"Look, I know he's stolen a few things here and there. But it's because he's hungry," Sammy tried to explain, thinking that surely even someone like Lindsay would understand that nobody should go without food.

Coming down the steps, Lindsay paused so that she was one step higher than Samantha. Her eyes were level and cool, even distant. "Sammy, you should really do yourself a favor. People around here had all but forgotten about you and your money-laundering father in the time you were gone. You waited a long time to come back, and you did it under a different name. You could have completely started over here in Sunny Cove, but you're falling right back into your old habits of hanging out with people that nobody else wants to have anything to do with."

"Listen, Austin really isn't a bad guy. He's been in some trouble, sure, but you would be too if you couldn't afford to feed yourself. I think a job would really make a big change in his life. He could make some extra money and use it to buy food instead of taking it. It would also really help him with socializing and working on his people skills." Sammy was desperate to make this work, but she hoped that it was showing through as determination more than anything. "I'm not asking you to let him come into your house or do anything that might make you uncomfortable. I'm just talking about little tasks like picking up trash or fallen sticks. You can pay him whatever you can afford."

Lindsay pushed past her and headed down the sidewalk toward her driveway. She gestured with one hand toward her yard, her rings sparkling in the early morning sunlight. "It's not a matter of the money. I've already got the best lawn team in the county."

"Or if you know someone else who might need his services. Even if there's a place alongside the highway that you'd like to sponsor where he could pick up trash..." Sammy knew she was probably selling this too hard, but she just had to find some way to make this work.

Reaching her little red BMW, Lindsay turned around and glared at Sammy. "Listen to me very carefully, because I don't want to have to repeat this again. I am not letting that lowlife criminal anywhere near me or the things I own, and I'm not putting my name or money behind any other project he wants to do. He might not have all the same advantages the rest of us do, but he made his decisions in life. Now he gets to live with them." She clicked the remote on her key ring pointedly.

Sammy didn't feel that was a fair assessment of Austin's situation at all, but Lindsay was about to jump in her car and speed away, and they still had more to talk about. "Okay, fine. I'll find someone else. But I was also wondering if you've seen or heard from Heather since the night of the party. We all know about the bloody piece of her costume, and it seems that she's missing."

Lindsay opened her car door and sighed. "This is exactly what I'm talking about, Sammy. You came back home and started hanging out with people like Heather again. I shouldn't have to remind you that she's never been particularly well-liked, not then and not now. It's not a shock to me if someone finally couldn't stand her any longer and decided to do something about it."

"What do you mean?" Sammy pressed. "Can you think of someone who would be upset with her?"

"Who wouldn't be?" Lindsay threw her hands in the air. "She was always mouthing off and causing trouble. And with the places she goes and the kind of people she hangs out with? She's just asking to become a statistic. If I were you, I wouldn't get involved before the same thing happens to you."

"But did you see anything suspicious at all? At the party or earlier in the day?"

"No." Lindsay's eyes were hard as emeralds now. "I don't

know anything for certain. But if I were you, I'd check with that no-good boyfriend of hers. He's from the wrong side of the tracks, he gets into just as much trouble as Heather does, and the two of them were constantly fighting. Good luck, I guess, but I've got to get going." She got into the driver's seat and slammed the door, zooming backwards out of the driveway.

Sammy watched her go, feeling dejected. She hadn't really expected someone like Lindsay to help her, but it would have been nice if she could have at least gotten a little information out of her. Stuffing the business card back in her pocket, she headed back to her car.

6

LET RISE

S canning down her list of people from the party, Sammy saw that she already had Billy York written down. He was the most obvious suspect, but he was the one who intimidated her the most. Sammy had only hung out with him when he had tagged along with Heather back in school, and she hadn't seen him at all since she had returned to Sunny Cove. He was known for being a bit wild and quite impetuous, lashing out when people angered him and not thinking about the consequences. Sammy had hoped she would be able to get some sort of lead on what had happened to Heather without having to talk to him, but Lindsay's statement was making her think otherwise. She still had a little bit of time before she had to be at work, and even though she would end up a bit behind on her baked goods for the day, she headed to the south side of town.

Several trailer parks had been established here, down near the river where the land was known to flood occasionally.

Most of them were decently maintained, with those closest to the water in the worst disrepair. If there was any place in town that could use Austin's help, it was this one. Trash skittered along in the breeze like small creatures escaping from predators, and several of the trailers had piles of broken toys and lawn equipment near one corner or under the porch. Sammy had looked up the address on her smartphone and now skimmed past the various streets, each one leading into a different park. She noted that the names on the signs were far more hopeful than the area looked, listing streets such as Magnolia, New Hope, and Sunshine. She turned onto one named Apple Tree and began checking the numbers on the trailers for the correct one.

Billy's trailer was at the very end of the street, with the back of it facing the muddy banks of the river. Sammy wouldn't have admitted it to anyone, but her heart raced with apprehension as she got out of her car this time. What if Billy had done something terrible to Heather? Would he attack Sammy for suspecting him? This was probably the worst neighborhood in Sunny Cove, and she had driven over here on a whim without even telling anyone where she was going. She didn't want to be in the same position as Heather.

But Sammy reminded herself that God would take care of her. Even if she didn't make it to church every Sunday morning, God wasn't going to just abandon her. Everything would be all right, and it was early morning. Terrible things didn't happen to people at that time of day.

She climbed the shaky steps to the front door, noting the plant pot near the door that had been used as an ash tray. The screen door creaked loudly when she opened it, and her heart jumped up into her mouth as she lifted her fist to knock.

Sammy listened carefully, expecting the sound of a dog barking or a TV blaring. But there weren't even any footsteps heading toward the door, and she knocked again. Was Billy a late sleeper? She supposed she would find out soon enough.

But when there was still no answer, she pulled her jacket a little tighter around herself and turned back to her car, only to find Sheriff Jones standing at the bottom of the steps. He watched her with a careful curiosity in his eyes. "Good morning," he said slowly. "Mind if I ask what you're doing here?"

Sammy immediately felt defensive. "I didn't know it was a crime to knock on someone's door."

"I never said it was, but I'm here because I have business here. I sure hope you don't." He leaned on the railing next to the stairs.

She knew exactly what he meant. Jones had told her specifically that she wasn't to look into Heather's disappearance, and yet here she was at Heather's boyfriend's house. "I do, actually. I'm trying to help Austin find some odd jobs. I realized nobody is going to want to hire him on as of yet, but there's no reason why he can't do some yard work." Sammy stepped slowly down the stairs until she stood on the makeshift walkway, and now she had to look up into the sheriff's eyes.

His gaze was harder than usual. "I know you don't want to hear this, but I don't think you'll have much more luck getting him employment like that. It's nice of you, but people have already formed their opinions about him. Even if you can get him some work, Billy York is probably the last person who's going to be able to hire him."

"Why is that?"

"Just look around," Sheriff Jones pointed out. "The people who live here don't stay because they like the scenery. Billy doesn't have a lot of extra money to go around, and I hear his mom has been sick as well. You're better off talking to folks on the other side of town."

"I tried that earlier this morning," Sammy admitted. "I didn't have much luck, but I'm not giving up yet."

"For what it's worth, even though I don't think it will work, I still hope it does." Jones' face softened a little as he looked at her, and Sammy noticed once again just how handsome he was. He had broad shoulders that filled out his uniform nicely.

"Thanks. I know you probably don't want me to ask you this, but have you found out anything about Heather? I've been so worried about her, and I know her mom has been too."

Jones sighed and glanced up at the trailer. "That's why I'm here, actually. Heather's car was found on the side of the highway on the east side of town. It was off down a shallow hill and into the tree line, so that's why nobody had found it until one of my officers happened to see it earlier this morning."

Sammy's entire body tensed. "And Heather?"

"No sign of her." Jones shook his head. "There's some blood on the steering wheel and some signs of a scuffle."

"And what does that have to do with Billy?" The inside of Sammy's mouth tasted metallic from all the adrenaline running through her system.

Jones shrugged. "We don't know for sure yet. I've been working my way down the list of people who were at the party, and a few of them have said they saw Billy getting in Heather's car on that night while it was still at Hewitt's house. But since everyone was in costume, it's not concrete enough evidence to really go on." His shoulders sagged slightly. "I'm sorry. She's your friend, and I can see I'm upsetting you. I shouldn't have told you any of this."

"No, it's okay. Really." Sammy turned away to swipe at the tears that were clinging to her lashes. "I want to know, even if it's hard. Do you think Billy was capable of doing something to her?"

The sheriff opened his mouth to speak but shut it again. He thought about it a moment before replying. "I don't want to say. The crime scene guys were all over the car this morning, so we'll find out soon enough if Billy's prints are on the car. It's no secret that we have them on file at the station, so it'll be easy enough to compare them. But even if they are, it doesn't necessarily mean he's guilty. The two of them dated a lot, and it would make sense that Billy had been in the car before."

This was something Sammy hadn't really thought about. "I guess that makes things pretty difficult to decipher."

"It would be a lot easier if I could find someone who actually knew something. Right now, I just have speculations and hearsay," Sheriff Jones admitted. "But I promise I'm working on it. And do me a favor, and don't say anything to anyone about what I just told you. It's supposed to be confidential until we know more."

"What about her mom?" Sammy knew that Jones had already stepped over the line by opening up to her, and she didn't want to abuse that, but Valerie was so concerned.

His brow creased. "I already talked to her. I don't think knowing helped, to be honest. I've got to get back on the road, and I suggest you do as well."

She nodded, but she couldn't quite let him go. "Sheriff Jones, are you sure there isn't anything I can do to help?"

He smiled, a handsome look on his tanned face. "You are one determined woman, you know that? But no, I really don't need any assistance from the public. I don't want everyone in Sunny Cove thinking they can run out into the streets and become vigilantes and private investigators. I'll let you do your job at the diner, and you can let me do my job at the station."

"Okay," she relented, even though she didn't quite like his answer. "You should come in some time for a cinnamon roll. They've been selling like crazy, but I can save you one if you'd like." Sammy wasn't quite sure what had made her say that. It sounded so forward, much bolder than she would normally be. Maybe it was what Helen had said about what a good man Sheriff Jones was, and it couldn't hurt to be friends with him even if she wasn't ready for more than that.

He gave her another of those winning smiles as he opened the door to his car. "I'll do that. Thanks."

7

ROLL OUT THE DOUGH

"There you are!" Helen exclaimed when Sammy raced in the back door of Just Like Grandma's. "It's not like you to be late, and you can't exactly tell me that you got stuck in traffic since you live upstairs."

"I could this morning, since I was running some errands, but honestly I just lost track of time." Sammy never should have taken the side trip to Billy's trailer park. It took longer than she had anticipated, even though Billy wasn't home, but it had been impossible to resist at the time. "I'm sorry."

"That's all right. Just do me a favor and take the orders from the tables over there in the corner before you start baking. They've already been waiting for a while, and two extra minutes to wait for rolls or biscuits won't kill anybody."

Sammy did as she was asked. Even though Helen hadn't

seemed all that bothered by her late appearance, and she had never been late for work before, she found herself moving more quickly and putting all of her effort into her job as a way of making up for it. Helen gave her a few looks throughout the day but didn't say anything about it.

When her midafternoon break came around, Sammy quickly untied her apron and hung it on a peg by the back door. "I'm going to run an errand while I'm on break, but I'll be right back."

Helen put one hand on her ample hip and looked at Johnny, the cook. "You see this? She comes in here, performs better than any waitress I've ever hired, gets the whole town addicted to her baking, and then she suddenly starts showing up late and running away every chance she gets."

Johnny, who never said much, simply shook his head.

"I don't suppose this would have anything to do with Austin, would it?" Helen queried. "You know I fully support what you're doing, but I don't want it to affect your work."

"I'm just going to talk to one person," Sammy promised. "I can't stop thinking about it, and I didn't have any luck this morning. I won't go over my break."

"You sure won't," Helen warned, but there was a glint of humor in her dark eyes. "Go on with you, then, or else I'll make Johnny get out on the floor and start taking orders."

The cook had been flipping a few burgers and toasted

cheese sandwiches on the grill, but he paused and to give his boss a startled look.

Helen laughed. "Don't worry, honey. I haven't tortured you like that yet, and I don't plan to. But you'd better hope that Sammy pays attention to her watch today."

With a smile, Sammy ducked out the back and walked down the alley before turning up toward Main Street. She crossed the road and walked into the front door of a building whose arched windows and intricate brickwork indicated how long it had been standing in downtown Sunny Cove. A large desk sat squarely in front of the door in the lobby, at which a young blonde woman was tapping frantically at the screen of her phone. "Can I help you?" she asked without looking up.

"I was wondering if Mr. Hewitt is available." Sammy realized she should have made an appointment. Someone like Rob Hewitt probably had his days booked solid, considering he was the head of the biggest law firm in town. But he was also the next person on her list of people at the party, and Sammy knew he didn't work far from the café. That would make it pretty easy to talk to him even when she only had a short amount of time.

The secretary still didn't look up from her phone. "Do you have an appointment?"

"No," Sammy replied, "but I just wanted to talk to him for a moment about something. It doesn't have anything to do with a legal case, if that makes any difference."

"Just a sec." The girl hammered a few more times on her phone before finally setting the device down. "What did you say your name was?" She reached for the handset to the landline just to her right.

"Samantha Baker."

The girl pushed a few buttons and muttered into the phone, listening and nodding, and then she hung up. She looked tired and bored as she turned back to Sammy. "He says you can go in for a minute, but he's got a consultation set for three o'clock. You'll have to make it quick."

Sammy wondered if those words had come from the attorney or if the secretary had provided them on her own, but she could work with them either way. "Thank you. Where's his office?"

The secretary gestured vaguely to a hallway that opened up behind her. "Last one on the left." She had already picked up her cell phone and was tapping furiously at the screen again.

"Thanks." Sammy headed down the hall, hoping this visit would be more fruitful than the other two she had already made that day.

Rob was seated behind his desk, dressed in a fine suit in dark blue instead of a green and brown Robin Hood costume. He looked up as she came in and immediately stood, reaching out his hand to shake hers. "It's nice to see you again, Sammy. I really am sorry if I was rude to you the other night. You were wearing the same costume as Lindsay, so I thought you were her."

Sammy didn't need yet another reminder that she had accidentally copied the most popular girl in school. "That's okay. These things happen. And I'm sorry to bother you. I was just wondering if you might have a few free minutes."

"Have a seat." He gestured at the leather chair in front of his desk. It was nice, but it was still nothing compared to the cushioned chair on rollers that he sat in. "What can I do for you? I don't have time to do a full consultation, but I can discuss a few things with you and then Stacey can find time for an appointment."

"No, I don't need anything like that at the moment." She bit the side of her lip. Sammy was going to start off talking about Austin, as she had previously, but the party had already been mentioned. "I'm sure that Sheriff Jones has already asked you, but do you know anything about what might have happened to Heather?"

Rob's face had been open and pleasant when she first walked in, but it darkened visibly as he picked up a pen on his desk and rapidly clicked the button on top of it several times. "Why are you asking me?"

"I'm asking everyone I know, to be honest." He clearly didn't like this line of questioning, and she had to get him to calm down a little so he would talk to her. "I know the sheriff's department is working on it, but I can't just let something like this go. I want to know that I'm doing something to help."

"Then I suggest you talk to that boyfriend of hers," Rob advised. "The two of them were always arguing, and I understand that's exactly what they were doing on the night of the party. They didn't even bother hiding it."

"I've heard that," Sammy admitted. "I don't know him all that well. I don't really even know Heather anymore, but I'm starting to. I just hope the sheriff can get this all sorted out."

"I'm sure he will. Is there anything else I can do for you?" Rob was clearly done with the subject of Heather and Billy.

"Actually, yes." Sammy briefly explained what she was trying to do for Austin. "Could you use him at all?"

Rob sat back in his chair, scratching at his chin. "It's an interesting idea, and I have to applaud you for it. I don't think anyone else has tried to solve Austin's problems like that. While there's no guarantee it would work, it's probably a lot better than just letting him run around stealing things. But I do have one major concern. Who's going to supervise Austin and make sure he gets the work done? If I hire him to clean up my business front, I can't also take time out of my day to stand out there and watch him."

"I've got that covered," Sammy replied instantly. "I'll be with him every step of the way. It's my hope that he'll eventually get to the point where he can do some of these jobs on his own, but right now he's going to need some guidance. I'll just make sure he does the work when I'm available."

Rob's attitude was completely different now than it had been when he had been talking about Heather, and he almost seemed excited about this Austin idea. "You know, if you *really* want to help him, you're going to need more of a long-term solution. Realistically, you're not going to be able to be with him all the time and constantly finding jobs for him, and it's not fair that you should have to use up all your free time."

"You're probably right," Sammy admitted, even though she didn't want to. "But I really don't mind. I used to volunteer a lot when I lived in New York, and I think it's good for the soul."

"But not for the checkbook," Rob countered. "Still, I think it's the start of something good. In the meantime, Austin has my permission to come pick up trash along the sidewalk and the little strip of grass here in front of the office."

"Oh, thank you!" Sammy stood up so quickly that she nearly knocked her chair over. "He's going to be so excited when he hears about this."

Rob shook her hand and gave her a casual smile. "No problem. I'll keep my eyes open for any other opportunities for him, but think about what I said. He's going to need more than just odd jobs if he's going to be able to sustain himself."

"I will. Thanks again!" Sammy headed quickly back to Just Like Grandma's. Her break was almost over, so her visit with Rob had taken up all of her time, but it had been worth it. She tried to shove his concerns to the back of her mind, because the most important thing right now was that Austin would get his first job. Yes, he was going to need more of them. Yes, it was going to be difficult for her to constantly be finding him new work and always having to supervise. But maybe if the uncle could get in on this, it wouldn't be so bad. She would address those matters later.

8

FORM ROLLS ON A BAKING SHEET

The next day was a much colder one, but at least the wind had died down somewhat. After a full day of schlepping trays and plates, wiping tables, and sweeping floors—not to mention all of her normal baking—Sammy gathered up several trash bags and two pairs of disposable gloves. Eventually, it would be nice if Austin could get one of those long trash pick-up tools, but the old-fashioned way would have to work for now. There was no point in him spending money he didn't yet have.

Austin came bursting into the diner just as Helen was headed to the front to turn off the open sign. In his usual mismatched style, he wore a pair of navy blue sweatpants, a bright green t-shirt, and a red hooded jacket. A grungy brown coat had been pulled over the rest of the ensemble. "Sammy! It's today!" He spread his arms out to each side.

She had to laugh at his exuberance. If only everyone was

so excited about work. He had been on the moon when she had given him the good news the previous afternoon, and he had been eager to get to work right away. "It certainly is. I'll be ready in just a few minutes."

"And you're going to be with me the whole time?" He looked slightly apprehensive all of a sudden.

"I sure am. I'll take you over there, and I'll stay with you, and then I'll take you home." It would make for a bit of a late evening, and they would be lucky to get it all done before dark now that it was getting closer to winter, but she had already made a vow to do everything she could for him. "Have you had any dinner?"

He shook his head.

Sammy wanted to shake hers back in disappointment. She didn't yet know all the circumstances surrounding Austin's situation, but she was very curious where his parents were and why he was living with this uncle who couldn't even afford to feed them. Instead, she dished out the last of the soup of the day and gave it to him with a biscuit. "Eat that up. You can't work on an empty stomach."

Austin eagerly did as he was told while Sammy finished cleaning up the diner. When the last customer was gone, she locked the front door and took him out the back.

The lights were still on at Hewitt's office, shedding squares of yellow light out on the sidewalk. "Okay, Austin.

We'll start here on the corner, and we can go all the way down to that lamp post." Sammy handed him a pair of gloves and shook out a garbage bag.

"Wabash, Indiana, was the first American city to use electric street lights," Austin responded.

"Now let's hope those electric lamps give us enough light to get this completed," Sammy said with a smile. "Mr. Hewitt said he's going to pay you twenty dollars. What do you think you'll do with the money?"

"Hamburgers," Austin replied as he bent down to retrieve a fast food wrapper. "Lots of hamburgers."

"That could be good. You could buy a couple of hamburgers, and then you could use the rest of the money to buy peanut butter and bread. You could make a lot of sandwiches out of that." Sammy suddenly realized that Austin's job was going to turn into a second job for her. She not only had to find him the work and make sure he got it done, but the poor boy was probably going to need help figuring out how to spend the money as well. Austin didn't know that it was better to go the store and buy groceries that would last a while instead of just eating out, and it would seem like a waste if she didn't help him with this.

"Should I get the trash in the gutter?"

"I think that would be a good idea. You want Mr. Hewitt to know you can do a good job." Sammy stepped along with him as he hunted down cigarette butts, old lottery tickets, and crumpled papers. "If we can get more jobs for you, what else do you think you might buy?"

"Gloves for Uncle Mitch. His have holes in them. Or pay for the heat."

This gave her pause. "You don't have heat in your house?"

"Sometimes. Sometimes no."

The more time she spent with him, the more Sammy was learning about Austin's home life. She desperately wanted to ask him more about his background, but she hadn't figured out yet just how much he could handle discussing. Austin was having fun picking up trash, and she didn't want to upset him. "Do you think Uncle Mitch would help you on some of these jobs? Maybe drive you where you need to be and stay until you're done?"

"Uncle Mitch works at the car wash sometimes."

"I see." But Sammy wasn't sure that she did. It was hard to get any information out of Austin, and she had a feeling it would take quite a few questions before she finally got the answer she was looking for. "Do you think I could talk to your Uncle Mitch when I take you home?"

Austin shrugged and continued his work.

When they had finished, Sammy directed Austin to tie up the bag and put it in a nearby dumpster while she invited Rob outside to see his work. "Well, that's pretty good,"

Rob said as he surveyed the street front, looking genuinely impressed. "How much of this did you do?" he muttered to Sammy.

"None of it," she replied honestly. "All I did was hold the bag."

"Here you go." The lawyer pulled a twenty-dollar bill out of his pocket and handed it to Austin. "You deserve it. I much prefer this to the way it normally is. You can come back next week and do it again."

"Oh, boy!" Austin held the cash up in the air like a trophy. "I will. Right, Sammy?"

"Yes, we certainly will. Thanks, Rob. I know it means a lot."

He nodded, but he glanced at Austin and then back at her. "Can I talk to you for a second?"

"Give me just a second, Austin, and then I'll take you home." She and Rob walked a few paces away, and she hoped he wasn't going to be upset with anything Austin had done. "What's up?"

"I just thought I would check with you and see if you had heard anything else about Heather. I know I kind of snapped at you about it yesterday, but it's disturbing to know that someone we went to school with might be missing. It's even more disturbing to think that the police might not be doing everything they can about it."

"I think they are. Sheriff Jones assured me of that." She'd had her doubts as well, but Sammy wasn't the kind of person to cast aspersions on someone. And Sheriff Jones seemed to genuinely care about the case.

Rob looked solemn. "Heather and I didn't always get along well, but I'm sure just about anyone you talk to will have a similar story. Even so, I hope she's okay."

"I do, too. And I'll let you know if I find out anything pertinent." Sheriff Jones had asked her not to say anything about finding Heather's car, and she was going to do her best to keep her promise. After all, it wasn't solid evidence yet.

She told Rob to have a good evening, and she and Austin walked back to where her car was parked behind Just Like Grandma's. She couldn't help but wonder about Rob's reactions when talking about Heather. Yesterday, he hadn't seemed inclined to discuss the matter at all and had almost seemed angry. Today, he was showing genuine concern. The inconstancy made her wonder if Rob had any connection with Heather's disappearance. Sammy had only chatted with him for a few minutes, and there was no telling what the party host had been doing before she had found him at the drinks table.

"Can we clean over there?" Austin interrupted her thoughts, pointing down the street to the parking lot of a convenience store that certainly looked like it could benefit from his assistance.

"No, Austin. We can't do anything until we have

permission from the people who own the land." Apparently, knowing he could clean up in front of Hewitt's office again the next week wasn't enough for Austin, and Sammy smiled. She was glad this had been a good experience for him. "Let's get you home."

Austin lived near the river, not quite to the trailer park that Sammy had visited before. She pulled up into his driveway, and though she knew Austin was capable of getting in the door by himself, she decided this was the perfect opportunity to talk to Uncle Mitch herself.

He met them at the front door of the shabby house, his back slightly stooped as he leaned heavily on the doorway. He gave Sammy a suspicious glare. "I don't know what he did, ma'am, but you let me know if he's bugging you. I know my boy here gets himself into a lot of trouble."

"No, he's not in any trouble at all," she assured him with a smile. "He was out doing some work, that's all."

Mitch looked from her to Austin and back again. "Work? The boy can't work."

"I can!" Austin held up his twenty-dollar bill. "See? We can go to the store now."

The old man shook a finger at him. "Boy, if you're stealing again, you're going to be in a lot of trouble."

Sammy wanted to diffuse this situation before it became a problem. "I don't think I've officially introduced myself. I'm Sammy Baker, and I work down at Just Like

Grandma's. Could I come in and talk to you for a minute?"

"I know who you are." The heavy sigh that he heaved made her think he would say no, but he nodded and held the door open for her. Sammy noted the shabby carpet, the old, rickety furniture, and the plastic taped over the windows against the breeze. It was chilly inside, but Mitch didn't seem to notice as he lowered himself into an old recliner and gestured at her to speak.

"I know that Austin has gotten into some trouble in the past, but I thought a few odd jobs might put some money in his pocket and keep him from breaking the law. It always seems to be food that he's stealing, which has me concerned for him. He did a wonderful job of cleaning up in front of an attorney's office today, and I'd like to talk with you and see if you might be able to take him to some of these jobs, as well."

Mitch ran a stiff hand through the remaining waves of his white hair and glanced at Austin. "Why don't you go make sure your room is clean?" Austin trotted off down the hallway, and Mitch waited until he was out of earshot before he said anything else. "He was telling me about all this, but I wasn't sure if I could believe him. He's always saying all sorts of crazy things. It's a nice idea, but I don't want to get his hopes up. I know how people feel about him in this town, and there aren't going to be very many who are willing to have him around, much less pay him to be there."

"He's really a wonderful person," Sammy replied. "I think

people just need a chance to get to know him apart from the times they've had to call the police on him. Give it some time. I don't mind helping him find these jobs. He did wonderfully today, and I think he'll have even more potential if you're able to drive him to complete these tasks."

Mitch heaved another sigh that seemed to deflate his body. "I'll try. Lord knows, the poor boy is going to need some way to take care of himself once I'm gone. His parents didn't want anything to do with him once they found out he wasn't quite right. They were going to put him up for adoption, but I couldn't stand the idea of him just living in the system for the rest of his life. I don't even know where my no-good sister and her husband are these days."

"That was very kind of you," Sammy choked out. She'd had no idea, and the story brought instant tears to her eyes. "I think they're the ones missing out."

For the first time, Mitch offered her a slight smile. "So do I. But the rest of Sunny Cove doesn't see him that way. I'm doing the best I can, but I'm old and I'm tired. There's just not much of me left to go around."

Sammy was beginning to realize that the problem was so much more than just Austin. It was Mitch, too, but it was also their circumstances. The web of poverty was a complicated one. "I understand. I just want him to get a fair chance. Is it all right if I continue to get these jobs for him?" She realized she should have asked Mitch first before she had set all of this up, but it was too late now.

Mitch nodded. "Of course. I think it's good for him, but I just hope he's not wasting your time. I'll talk to him about behaving himself while he's with you, too. I want this to go well."

"Wonderful." Sammy stood. "It's late, and I don't want to intrude on your evening any longer than I already have. Austin does have another job lined up with Mr. Hewitt next week. Is it all right if I say goodbye to him?"

The old man waved her down the hallway.

When she found his room, Sammy was surprised to see that it was so neat and orderly. The carpet needed a good vacuum, but the clothes all hung neatly in the closet and books were lined up on the shelves. The room had a childlike quality to it, since Austin had a Batman comforter and several stuffed animals on his bed, but he'd only had a few minutes, since his uncle had sent him, to make sure his room was clean. "Do you always keep it so tidy in here?" she asked.

Austin turned from a shelf of soldier figurines and smiled at her. "I've been practicing. You said I was going to be cleaning, so I wanted to make sure I could."

"You certainly can." Sammy realized that it would only take a little bit of training to make Austin into an amazing employee. She would have to find the right people to give him the right chance, and that would probably take some time, but seeing his room let her know that he was capable of so much more than just picking up trash on the side of the street. "I'm getting ready to leave. You make sure you spend that money wisely, okay? Talk to your Uncle Mitch about it. Don't just go down to the store and buy a bunch of candy."

He shook his head emphatically. "Nope. Sandwiches and stuff."

"That's right. And I'll let you know as soon as we find more jobs, okay?"

"Okay, Sammy. Bye!" He started playing with his figurines again.

When she was back in her car, Sammy knew there was an opportunity she couldn't resist. She was only a few blocks away from Billy's house, and she had yet to find any good leads on Heather. Turning down his road and hoping she wouldn't regret it, Sammy was knocking on his door only a few minutes later.

This time, it swung open almost immediately. The porch light had just come on against the pending darkness, and Billy's slim face stared at her with wild eyes.

"Hi, Billy. I don't know if you remember me, but—"

"Sammy! Please tell me you know something about Heather!" He leapt out onto the porch, goose pimples immediately standing out on his arms against the chilly wind that had picked up once again.

She shook her head. "No, I'm afraid I don't. But that's why I came here. I wanted to see if you knew anything."

Billy's eyes narrowed, and he looked down his nose at her suspiciously. "Why?"

"Because the two of you were together a lot, and I'd like to find out where she is," Sammy replied honestly.

"So would I." He had calmed down again, but that feral look still lurked in the back of his eyes. "I knew that party was a bad idea. She never did well when she was around the people we went to school with."

Sammy tipped her head. She hadn't thought about that before, but she hadn't been around Heather enough as an adult to know. "Why is that?"

He gave a derisive snort. "You don't remember all the trouble she caused? She was always putting her nose where it didn't belong. Not to mention all the problems with Rob and Lindsay."

"What do they have to do with it?" Sammy pulled her jacket a little tighter around herself, wondering why Billy didn't let her in. But if the dilapidated state of the outside of the trailer was also reflected on the inside, then maybe she did know why.

"That was the worst part! That whole thing about Rob breaking up with Lindsay and asking out Heather instead?" Billy prompted.

Sammy frowned, trying to remember. But her time in high school had been so taken up with thoughts of her father, who was rotting in jail for crimes he didn't commit, that she hadn't paid a lot of attention to anything else happening around her. "I vaguely remember it."

"It was a pretty big deal. He asked Heather out, but when everyone else heard about it, he started backing off and saying it had all been a joke. He was embarrassed to be seen with her, and he went running right back to Lindsay. They still didn't work out, but that didn't matter. It was exactly what Heather *didn't* need right then, and it's still affecting her. She's never felt like she was good enough. I know it's all just silly stuff that happened back in high school, but trust me, it's still happening."

"But why would she care about what Rob or Lindsay think of her now, if she's got you?" Sammy had no idea that this was happening in Heather's mind, and it bothered her. They had talked multiple times since Sammy had arrived back in Sunny Cove, and it seemed like the sort of thing that would come up. The only thing that Heather had mentioned was that they had been engaged for a short period.

Billy dug a pack of cigarettes out of his pocket and lit one, blowing the smoke off to the side. "We love each other, but we've never gotten along very well. My guess is that she's having another one of her episodes."

"Episodes?" Sammy had been hoping to come here for new clues, but she was only getting more questions.

He shrugged and flicked his cigarette in the air. "Sometimes Heather just likes to disappear for a while, you know? I think it gets her some of the attention she craves. She wants someone to come and find her and beg her to come back home, because it makes her feel special."

"I didn't know. Are there any places where I should be looking?" It suddenly registered with Sammy that even though she and Heather had hung out a little bit, she really had no idea where the other woman liked to go, what she liked to do, or what people she hung out with. That could certainly be helpful.

Billy's shaggy brown hair ruffled in the breeze as he took another drag from his cigarette. "I've already made all the rounds. I've checked all the bars she and I used to go to. I've asked everyone I know." He ground his smoke out in the flower pot and scratched his forehead, not looking up. "I love her, you know. Even though we aren't a good match and I know she still wants to be with Rob."

Sammy took a deep breath, knowing she was about to do something she shouldn't. Sheriff Jones had entrusted her with some information, and she wasn't supposed to share it. But she needed to get a clearer picture of what was going on here. "Listen, I heard that Heather's car was found off the side of the highway, a little ways out of town. Some people are saying they saw you in her car that night. Do you know what any of that is about?"

Billy's dark eyes, which had been soft and sad as he spoke of Heather, were suddenly hard. He took a step backwards, toward the door of his trailer, and he watched Sammy carefully. "Well don't look at me! I don't know how it got there!"

"But were you in her car on the night of the party?"

"Only for a second!" he spluttered. "We'd had a fight, and she ran off. I thought about leaving the party, but I wasn't about to let Rob find her and start consoling her. So I hung out. But I didn't know where she went, and I checked her car to see if she had gone to lay in the back seat. She does that when she's had too much to drink, you know." His gaze darted around the trailer park, looking at everything but Sammy.

"But did you see her again after your fight?" Sammy pressed.

Headlights came zooming down the road, cutting off their conversation as they both turned to squint into the bright beams. They remained on as the vehicle pulled up behind Sammy's, and Billy cursed under his breath when Sheriff Jones got out of the driver's door.

Sammy took a step back, suddenly feeling incredibly guilty. She had been told not to meddle, and now she had been caught red-handed.

Though Jones gave her a glaring look in the yellow glow from the porch light, it was Billy he was interested in. "William York, you're under arrest for the abduction of Heather Girtman."

Even in the late evening light, Sammy could see that all the color had drained from Billy's face. His lips went white as he leaned back against the door of his home. "What? Why?"

The sheriff took his handcuffs off his belt and gestured at Billy to hold his hands out in front of him. "Heather's purse was found in a bush not far from the party. It was missing the car keys, and your fingerprints were all over it. They were also in Heather's car."

"Of course they were!" Billy protested, the whites of his eyes showing as he goggled at the metal restraints on his wrists. "We had gotten back together, at least for a little while. I bet there were other fingerprints. Did you check for those? I'm innocent!"

Sheriff Jones escorted him down the shaky wooden stairs to the squad car. "Save it for your lawyer, Billy. I'm just doing my job." He put Billy in the car and shut the door before turning and looking pointedly at Sammy. "Do I even want to know what you're doing here?"

Putting her chin in the air and straightening her shoulders, Sammy cleared her throat to give herself an extra minute to think. "I told you that I needed to talk to Billy about some things."

He shook his head. "I don't believe you, Sammy, but I don't have time to deal with it right now. Just do me a favor and stay out of this before I end up having to figure out what happened to you, as well."

"But you've just arrested your suspect," she pointed out.

Jones tipped his head toward the car. "Suspect, yes. That doesn't mean he's the perpetrator, and I'd much rather be safe than sorry. Get in your car. I'm not leaving until I know you're out of here and on your way home."

As much as she appreciated his concern for her safety, Sammy didn't like being ordered into her vehicle. She wanted to be helpful to the case, even though she didn't know how to do it. But she obediently got back in her Toyota and drove out of the trailer park, heading home.

9

BAKE UNTIL GOLDEN BROWN

I t was fully dark by the time she arrived at her apartment over Just Like Grandma's. The heavy scent of cinnamon still hung in the air from the baking she had done earlier in the day, but it was no comfort to her at the moment. Billy had been arrested, but Sheriff Jones had made no mention of finding Heather. And he had mentioned that Billy was under arrest for the *abduction* of Heather, not the murder. That had to at least be a good sign, or maybe it was just what he had to say since a body hadn't been found yet.

Sammy made sure the door was securely locked behind her before she went around to each of the windows and ensured they were fastened as well. On the second story of a building located in the middle of downtown, she had always felt fairly safe. But there was a chance she had just been talking face-to-face with a criminal, and it made her nerves dance under her skin. She turned on the kettle and dug some herbal tea bags out of the cabinet.

The night seemed too solemn an occasion to just turn on the television and try to forget about what happened. And Sammy just wasn't the kind of person to stand back and let events unfold. She wanted to act, to be useful no matter what the situation. Jones had forbidden her from doing so, and it caused such a conflict inside her that she couldn't relax.

Instead, Sammy launched herself off the couch and headed across her apartment to the bedroom. There had been several boxes she still hadn't unpacked from her move, and she had stashed them under the bed. She pulled them out now, sliding them across the hardwood floor until she found the right one labeled "School Stuff." The cardboard was dented and beaten from going through several moves without ever being opened, but she knew it was time now.

Underneath a framed picture of her at her graduation and several academic certificates, Sammy found what she was looking for. Even though she hadn't looked at them in years, Sammy recognized the covers of her yearbooks instantly. Back when they had been new, and she had still been a little excited to have her friends sign the insides of the covers, Sammy had spent a lot of time carrying them around. It seemed like forever ago now as she picked up the one from her senior year and flipped through it.

The senior superlatives were on the very center page, grabbing her attention immediately. Rob and Lindsay were in one of the pictures, which declared them Most Likely to Get Married. Sammy gave a snort of laughter as she read the line, even though she and many of the other students had felt it to be true at the time.

Neither herself nor Billy were in the pictures on that page, but Heather was featured as Most Fun. Someone had posed her with a paper party hat and a noisemaker, her dark hair only coming down to her chin back in those days. With her heavy eyeliner and thick choker paired with a black dress, she had been the dictionary definition of a wild party girl who never really fit in. The other students had voted her as fun, but that was just because she was always at parties, looking for someone to pay attention to her.

Sammy turned several more pages, catching a few random snapshots of Rob and Lindsay sitting together at a basketball game, Heather making faces in the cafeteria, and even Billy hiding behind a book when he didn't want his picture taken. The more she thought about it, the more she remembered about the love triangle Billy had described. Could he really have acted violently out of jealousy? It wouldn't be the first time something like that had happened, and he had admitted to Sammy that he didn't want Rob consoling Heather after their fight.

What about Rob? He had acted strangely when Sammy had initially asked him about Heather, and that had made her wonder about him. But when he had talked to her the next night, after Austin had cleaned up in front of the attorney's office, he had seemed genuinely concerned for Heather. It could have been an act. Was Rob as interested in dating Heather as Heather was in him? The two of them were from completely different lives, different parts of town, and they would have made an odd couple.

And what about Lindsay? A triangle couldn't be a triangle without all three points. She clearly despised Heather, but she made a good point when she said that everyone did. And Sammy had seen Lindsay—talked to her even—after Heather had disappeared. So she wouldn't have had a chance to do anything to Heather.

Still, Sammy'd had enough of sitting around and reminiscing over old yearbooks. She had only talked to Lindsay once since the party, and it couldn't hurt to make another quick visit. It wasn't yet late enough to be completely inappropriate. She flew to her feet and to the door, but she had to stop and undo all the locks first. She laughed at herself for being so afraid as she got in her car and went across town.

All the lights were on, illuminating the big white house on the corner. Lindsay was slow to come to the door, answering with a huff. "What do you want?" she barked. Her makeup was still on for the day, but she had changed into designer yoga pants and a tunic. "Do you have any idea what time it is?"

"Only eight-thirty," Sammy responded with a smile. She stepped up to the threshold and over it, letting herself in. "We didn't get much of a chance to talk yesterday, since you were on your way to work, and I thought it would be a good idea if we took a little time to catch up." She glanced quickly around the living room. Everything here was perfect and pristine, from the white carpet to the leather furniture.

"Okay," Lindsay replied slowly. "But maybe there would be a better time to do this? I was getting ready to go to bed."

"So early? You have a lovely home, by the way. You must have done well for yourself." She noted that nobody else seemed to be home, which was interesting since there were so many lights on.

"Well enough, I guess. Look, I really don't have time for this. Can we do this some other time?" Lindsay pointedly glanced at her watch.

But Sammy knew she couldn't leave just yet. "I guess. I just need to use your restroom really quick."

Lindsay's mouth worked open and shut a few times before she finally relented. "I guess that's all right. It's down the hall."

Sammy headed in the direction Lindsay indicated, noting that there were quite a few doors that lined the hall. She felt guilty about doing it, but she quickly peeked behind each one as she made her way to the open bathroom door at the end. She found a linen closet, a spare bedroom, and an office. One of the doors was locked, but light showed in the crack underneath.

When she finally reached the bathroom, she was careful to close the door quietly so Lindsay wouldn't be suspicious of her snooping. She quickly checked through the medicine cabinet, not sure of what she was looking for. She found several bottles of weight loss pills, anxiety medicine, and herbal supplements, but none of those were any kind of solid evidence. Realizing this wasn't going to help as much as she thought, she flushed the toilet and ran the faucet to keep her cover story and headed back to the living room.

"Are you sure you don't have any time to talk?" she asked. "I thought it might be fun to sit down and go through some old yearbooks, catch up on where everyone is at these days."

"I think we're a little old for slumber parties. Just go." Lindsay marched to the door and emphatically opened it.

"Okay, I understand. I'll talk to you later!" Sammy headed home to think and to finish that mug of tea she had made. She needed it.

10

DRIZZLE WITH ICING

"You're sure about this?" Sheriff Jones leaned back in his desk chair and gave her a skeptical look. "It seems a little far-fetched."

"I know. And I know you don't want me involved, but I am whether you like it or not. Just please, at least explore the possibility."

"Very well," he sighed. Sammy watched as he picked up the phone and made a call. He hung up and glanced at her with tired eyes. "She'll be here soon. I suggest you work quickly. Lawson here will take you out to the house." He gestured to his right, where a lanky deputy was leaning against a desk.

He stood up at hearing his name. "Really, sir? No disrespect, but this is a wild goose chase."

"It may be, but it's one I'm ordering you to do. You'd better get going."

Sammy followed him quickly to his squad car, hoping beyond all hope that she was right.

When she and Lawson returned thirty minutes later, Sammy's throat tightened when she saw that Lindsay's little red BMW was parked in the station lot. She hung back in the lobby, listening through the open door.

"Is this going to take much longer?" Lindsay's voice demanded. She was being loud, and she would have been easy to understand even if Sammy hadn't been trying to eavesdrop.

"Yes, just a second." Sheriff Jones sounded bored. "Since I'm questioning you about a potential murder suspect, I have to fill out all the appropriate paperwork first."

Lawson stepped past Sammy and into the office, handing a packet of paper to Jones.

"Ah, yes. We're all settled now. You can see that I have a suspect behind bars right here behind me. But I need to question a few other folks, as well, before I can submit all of my evidence. Do you recognize this purse?"

Sammy wanted desperately to walk into the room and see the entire thing. But she knew she had to stay hidden to make this work. She had seen Billy there in the jail cell, and she knew the poor man was probably going crazy during this whole process.

"Yes, that's Heather's bag," Lindsay replied.

"And, I know this is a little disturbing, but I have a piece of clothing here that we believe belonged to the victim. I apologize, because it's a little bloody, but can you tell me if you know who it belongs to?"

Sammy very clearly remembered the scrap of Heather's costume that had been found, and she knew Jones was showing it to Lindsay at that moment.

"It must be part of Heather's costume. She wore that trashy pirate getup, and it would be hard to confuse it with anything else."

"Now, were you a witness to the altercation between Heather and Mr. York here?"

"I was. I couldn't hear most of it, because the party was pretty noisy, but they were definitely yelling at each other. He used some very inappropriate language, too."

"That doesn't make me a killer!" Billy hollered from his jail cell. "Or anything else for that matter! You've got to let me go!"

"Pipe down, unless you want to make the situation worse," Jones called to him. "And I should remind you that you can't afford a good lawyer."

"Is there anything else?" Lindsay asked impatiently. "I have things I need to do today."

"Just one more thing," Jones promised her. "A new piece of

evidence has come in just this morning, and I'd like to know what you think about it."

Sammy knew that was her cue. She turned to the woman she had brought with her. Several bruises dotted her face and arms, and her dark hair was matted and dirty. Still in the costume from the other night, she looked like a reject from the circus. She needed a bath, a nap, a meal, and possibly even a doctor, but she had already told Sammy that she could definitely do this. Sammy stepped aside to let Heather walk into the room.

"What?" Lindsay screeched.

Sammy stepped into the room just in time to see Lindsay shoot up from her seat in front of the sheriff's desk. She gaped at Heather for a split-second before making a beeline for the door, but Sammy was blocking her way. Looking desperately around the room like a caged animal and finding nothing but unformed men, she finally sagged back down into the chair.

"Heather!" Billy was reaching through the bars of his cell. "I'm so glad to see you!"

Heather crossed the room to touch his hand. "I am glad to be here."

"I think you owe everyone here a bit of an explanation," Jones said to Lindsay.

At first, Sammy didn't think the other woman was going to talk. But she must have known she was caught, because she simply pressed her hand to her forehead and began speaking. "I was really excited about the Halloween party. I really thought it was my chance to get back together with Rob for good this time. We had both tried dating other people, but I knew we were both single. I thought I had it in the bag until Heather showed up."

"She had her cute little costume on," Lindsay continued. "I had no idea she was coming, and I was so angry that she was there. It only made it worse that Rob was instantly staring at her and flirting with her. I tried to ignore it. But then Heather and Billy got into yet another fight, probably over something stupid, like always. She was crying, and I saw her go upstairs to fix her face, so I followed her."

"And why did you do that?" Jones asked quietly.

"So she could pick a fight with me," Heather volunteers. "I'd already had a few drinks, and then I was crying and upset from fighting with Billy. I wasn't prepared for someone to barge into the bathroom and start attacking me. She hit me in the nose and I fell backwards, tearing my costume. I guess that was enough for her for the moment, because she stormed out."

Jones leaned forward and folded his hands on his desk. "And there weren't any witnesses to this?"

Heather shook her head. "Nobody else was upstairs, and that's exactly why I had gone up there to fix my face instead of using the bathroom on the main floor. I was ready to leave the party, and I remembered Billy had said something about finding my bag earlier in the evening and hanging it up on a peg near the back door. I made it downstairs and outside, but I went out the back so nobody would see me. I got to my car but I realized I had dropped my purse, so I returned to the backyard to find it."

"That must have been when I came outside to see if I could find you," Billy volunteered from his cell. "The door was open and the dome light was on, so I came to see if you were in there passed out. I didn't see you, so I went back inside."

"We must have just missed each other," Heather confirmed. "I couldn't find my purse, and I didn't want to waste any more time on it. I went back to the car and drove off. I thought I would go to a bar I like over in Oak Hills, but about halfway there I realized I was too blitzed to be behind the wheel. I pulled off to the side, and that's all I remember."

"You passed out," Lindsay said miserably. "I left the party after our fight, too. One of my sorority sisters was having a party that night as well, and I thought I would go over there. I saw your car on the side of the road. The lights were still on, and you had only made it out the door before you passed out. I was so angry with you, but I don't really know what I was thinking when I put you in the back of my car and took you home. I guess I thought I was going to get some sort of revenge, but by the next morning I realized I didn't know what I was going to do with the woman I had locked in my basement."

"So you just let them pin it on me?" Billy demanded.

"I thought it would buy me some time, at least," Lindsay replied.

Jones finally stood up and came around the desk. "You're under arrest for the abduction of Heather Girtman. Do I need to cuff you to the chair while we fill out the paperwork, or are you going to cooperate?"

"I'll cooperate," she promised. "There's not much point in running, is there?"

"No, ma'am. Lawson, let Billy out, please."

The deputy opened the door to the cell and Billy rushed out, hugging Heather and looking positively elated.

Sammy smiled, too. She knew she would probably get an earful from Sheriff Jones later for sticking her nose into the case, but she would make it up to him with some fresh cinnamon rolls. Most importantly, Heather had been found and the real criminal was being dealt with. Everything was going to be all right.

11

SERVE HOT AND SHARE WITH FRIENDS

Sammy looked in the mirror, studying every aspect of her outfit. The dark blue dress and flats she had put on were dressy but not too fancy, and they should be just about right for church. Still, her stomach churned and she considered backing out, but she knew she couldn't today. She had someone else counting on her. She got in her car and set off.

Heather hopped in the passenger seat a few minutes later. She hadn't bothered to dress up very much, choosing a nice blouse with a pair of jeans, but she had toned down her wild makeup. "I'm not sure why I let you talk me into this."

Sammy handed her a small paper sack that contained a cinnamon roll. "I even brought breakfast, so you can't exactly complain."

"Not about that part," Heather admitted as she pulled out

the sticky bun. "Still, I considered calling you and pretending I was sick."

"We'll have fun," Sammy promised her.

The parking lot to the Sunny Cove Church was already getting full by the time they arrived, and services weren't set to start for another twenty minutes. Sammy parked near the back of the lot and took deep breaths in an effort to drive the butterflies out of her stomach.

Several others turned their heads when Sammy and Heather walked into the sanctuary, and Sammy had never felt more self-conscious. She quickly found them some seats near the back and pretended to flip through the hymnal.

"Maybe we should leave," Heather suggested. "I feel like I'm not wanted here."

"They're just surprised to see us," Sammy assured her, hoping it was true. "And we're here for ourselves, and for our own spiritual development. We only need to care about what God thinks, not what everyone else thinks."

Heather nodded, the conservative bun she had made of her hair bobbing along. "I guess you're right." She smiled at her friend. "I should let you know that Billy and I have made amends, but we've decided to just be friends for now. Neither one of us in interested in doing the on-again, off-again thing anymore. We care a lot about each other, but I need some time to rediscover myself and figure out what I want from life."

"I'm really proud of you," Sammy said, feeling her heart lift inside her chest. She had never set out to change Heather or make a difference in her life, but it seemed that the events of the last few days had done just that. "And what about Rob?"

"No." Heather shook her head. "Maybe someday, in the future, but not right now. I was going to tell you this morning, but I guess you already heard that I decided not to press charges against Lindsay?"

She had. It had shocked her a little at first, but she understood. "That was very generous of you."

"The sheriff thought so, as well. He still thought she needed to learn a lesson about right and wrong, so he made arrangements with the judge to order Lindsay to do fifty hours of community service." Her blue eyes sparkled. "Jones also put in a word to have those community service hours served alongside Austin, helping him with any jobs that he may have."

Sammy wanted to shriek with excitement. Sheriff Jones wanted to help Austin just as much as she did. But she wasn't going to make a fool of herself in church, especially since this was the first time she had been back since returning to Sunny Cove. "That's so exciting! Now I'll just have to find more jobs."

But she soon realized after the service that she didn't need to worry. Several worshipers approached her and greeted her in the fellowship hall, saying they had heard about what she was doing for Austin and that they wanted to help. Even the pastor said Austin could come pick up his yard anytime he was available.

As Sammy and Heather walked back to her car afterwards, Sammy turned around to look up at the steeple on top of the church. Sunbeams shone down through the cross, creating a beautiful picture and creating a sense of peace in her heart.

"Everything okay?" Heather asked, seeing her pause.

"Yeah," Sammy replied. "It really is."

Thank you so much for reading, *Rolling Out a Mystery*. We hope you really enjoyed the story. If so, leaving a review is a great way to let others know (reviews are such a great encouragement to our authors also!). Leave a Review Now!

Also, make sure to sign up to receive PureRead Donna Doyle updates at PureRead.com for more great mysteries, exclusive offers and news of our new releases. We love to surprise our readers and would love to have you as part of our reader family!

Much love, and thanks again,

Your Friends at PureRead

* * *

Sign Up For Updates:

http://pureread.com/donnadoyle

BROWSE ALL OF DONNA DOYLE'S BOOKS

http://pureread.com/donnadoylebooks

MORE BAKER'S DOZEN MYSTERIES...

Dying For Cupcakes

BOXSET READING ENJOYMENT

ENJOY HOURS OF CLEAN READING WITH SOME OF OUR BESTSELLING BOXSETS...

Here at PureRead we love to offer great stories and great value to our readers.We have a growing library of amazing clean read boxsets that deliver dozens of delightful stories in every bundle. Here are just a few, or browse them all and grab a bargain on our website...

Look for PureRead titles on Amazon or visit our website at
PureRead.com/boxsets

PureRead Clean Reads Box Set Volume II

PureRead Clean Reads Box Set Volume I

PureRead Christmas Stocking of Stories

Seasons of Regency Romance Boxset

PureRead Terri Grace Legacy Boxset

Rainbow Mountain Brides Boxset

Mega Amish Romance Boxset

Christian Love 21 Book Contemporary Romance Boxset

** BROWSE ALL OF OUR BOX SETS **

ABOUT PUREREAD

Thank you for reading!

Here at PureRead we aim to serve you, our dear reader, with good, clean Christian stories. You can be assured that any PureRead book you pick up will not only be hugely enjoyable, but free of any objectionable content.

We are deeply thankful to you for choosing our books. Your support means that we can continue to provide stories just like the one you have just read.

PLEASE LEAVE A REVIEW

Please do consider leaving a review for this book on Amazon - something as simple as that can help others just like you discover and enjoy the books we publish, and your reviews are a constant encouragement to our hard working writers.

LIKE OUR PUREREAD FACEBOOK PAGE

Love Facebook? We do too and PureRead has a very special Facebook page where we keep in touch with readers.

To like and follow PureRead on Facebook go to **Facebook.com/pureread**

OUR WEBSITE

To browse all of our PureRead books visit our website at PureRead.com